The Takeover

by

Lilian Marsland

authorHOUSE®

AuthorHouse™
1663 Liberty Drive
Bloomington, IN 47403
www.authorhouse.com
Phone: 1 (800) 839-8640

Published by AuthorHouse   03/13/2015

ISBN: 978-1-4184-2162-5 (sc)

Library of Congress Control Number: 2004092953

Print information available on the last page.

CHAPTER 1

Charlie left the stink of the fish-canning factory and wound his weary way home.

For six years, four of them as manager, he'd been doing the same thing day after day, six days a week.

He was tired of it, and he knew he was due for a change.

It was mid-July, and after a clammy, humid night, he walked out into a hot, sunny morning; he always enjoyed the walk home.

After being stuck in the factory all night, the morning air was fresh and revitalizing, even in the winter.

After walking for about twenty minutes, he reached the beginning of the long straight driveway, leading to his home.

It had once been an old run-down farmhouse.

His parents had bought it for a song and sunk all their savings into renovating it.

That was forty something years ago, in the days when materials were strong and dependable.

The spacious home had stood the test of time and the rough and tumbles of four rambunctious kids.

It stood on an acre of land, in an open rural setting, which always gave Charlie a great sense of freedom.

The original sturdy oak beams still existed, the floorboards creaked a bit in certain places, and the roof had been repaired a few times; but the house still had an old-fashioned, comfortable feeling about it.

As Charlie reached the front door, he could hear his mother's voice.

She was in one of her moods again.

Ma didn't take too kindly to the hot, sweltering weather.

It always made her cranky, especially when she didn't sleep well.

Of the four siblings, only Charlie and Josh remained at home.

Their father, John, a retired carpenter, was still an early riser, but ma was usually up before him, preparing breakfast, just as she had always done.

Charlie entered the house, and the wonderful, soothing smell of bacon cooking filled his nostrils. It made him realize how hungry he really was.

Josh was already sitting at the table eating.

"Morning, Ma. Morning, Josh," Charlie called cheerily.

Josh nodded as he consumed a mouthful of bacon.

"Hi, Charlie," ma replied wearily.

Charlie could see by the expression on her face that today was not one of her better days.

He knew his mother well, and he knew how to make her feel better.

She always responded to a little TLC. It never failed to do the trick.

"Come and sit down for a few minutes, ma," he said. "I'll massage your shoulders."

Years of habit and feeding her husband before he left for work prompted her to reply, "No son, I have to see to the breakfast." "Come on, ma, it'll only take five minutes."

Ma didn't need any more persuading.

She relaxed as she sank into the big, green, comfortable armchair in the large homely kitchen and closed her eyes.

He gently pressed his strong fingers into her neck and shoulders.

Charlie was the youngest of her four children.

He was understanding and sensitive, and they could almost read each other's thoughts.

One day, he'll make a good husband for some lucky girl, she thought, knowing that he wouldn't live at home forever.

"There you go, ma. how's that?" He hugged her.

"That's great, Charlie. I feel much better now," she said, smiling.

"Think I'll hit the shower before I eat, ma," he said.

Then his mother knew that she was in for a splash of Frank Sinatra.

Strains of "Strangers in the Night" echoed from the shower throughout the house.

Charlie had a nice voice, and she loved listening to him.

CHAPTER 2

Later, father and son sat down at the table.

Ma always ate last and alone, except on Sundays, when dad did the cooking.

While they were eating, dad flicked the TV on.

More news about gas prices going up, earthquake in Japan, temperatures soaring to the highest they had been for several years, and an unusual amount of large spiders noticed in various areas around Arizona. The species had not yet been identified.

"So what's unusual about spiders?" asked Charlie. "They're all over the place."

His dad laughed and agreed with him.

Charlie finished breakfast, and then went to bed to get some sleep.

An hour later, dad collected the mail.

"Nothing too exciting here, Jean," he said to ma, thumbing through some bills.

Then he found a letter from their eldest daughter, Sheena. Lots of news about their three grandchildren, now teenagers, and how their son-in-law, Tom, was faring in his contracting business.

They'd moved out to Nevada a couple of years before.

Sheena told them about one of the kids' friends being bitten by a large spider when he and his family were on vacation in Arizona. After the bite, he became quite ill.

Because the spider had not been identified, he could not be given an antidote.

It was thought that because he was young and strong, with a good immune system, he'd recover quickly.

Ma worried about Sheena.

She worried about all her kids, but Sheena most of all.

A few years before, her marriage had been in trouble, and things didn't look good.

She and Tom had finally patched things up and decided to start afresh in Nevada.

Everything appeared to be working out well.

The kids were enjoying their new life, and Sheena had found some part-time work in a bookstore.

Tom is a nice enough fellow as son-in-laws go, but in ma's eyes not good enough for Sheena.

She thinks he's a little too fond of the ladies.

Of course, she muses, he was Sheena's choice, and she loves him, so who is she to criticize?

John was in the shower, and Josh was working on his car before going to his temporary job as a waiter.

The clock on the wall quietly demanded to be heard, and the sound of silence was peaceful.

Suddenly, her thoughts and the tranquil stillness were interrupted by the persistent ringing of the telephone.

The caller was Alice, ma's other daughter. She usually phoned about once a month.

Alice was very pretty and well sought-after.

With one marriage down the tube, she just didn't know which way life was taking her.

She had trained as a beautician but had recently felt that she needed to do something more with her life.

Making people look good was fine but not fulfilling enough for her.

She decided to become a state-registered nurse.

Ma was glad about that, because it was her ambition many years ago to do the same thing.

Then she met John, and after a whirlwind courtship, they were married.

The kids soon came on the scene, and the rest is history.

Alice was bubbling over with news about the young, dark-haired doctor she had met.

Ma was her best friend, more like a sister, and she often confided in her.

Josh was a completely different kettle of fish.

His interests lay in the arts and acting.

Since his mid-teens, he'd attended drama school and had become a very competent actor.

Soon, he would be leaving for New York to star in a new play, which was due to begin in the autumn.

John and Jean were very proud of him and hoped they would be able to go see the play.

CHAPTER 3

WASHINGTON, D.C., THE WHITE HOUSE

One of the many issues the president and his advisors had to resolve was the continuance of nuclear testing.

The last U.S. nuclear testing had occurred months before, and the U.S. had finally decided to stop polluting the earth and the air we breathe in its quest for self-preservation.

Hundreds of thousands of desert creatures were annihilated, and millions of precious dollars went up into the atmosphere.

The government was still debating about other countries that continued testing after the U.S. had stopped, much to the disgust and concern of the world.

In the Arizona laboratory, Dr. Sam Mason was hard at work, forehead furrowed with concentration.

Dr. Richard Clark walked in.

"Any break through yet, Sam?" He asked.

"Nothing so far," answered Sam.

"This is priority. I've got all my technicians working on it day and night, but so far, nobody's come up with anything. It's so damned puzzling,"

More and more people were seeking medical advice after being bitten by mystery spiders.

A couple of the spiders had been killed and brought to the lab for identification, which was proving difficult.

These spiders were different from any species that Sam knew of.

They had two front legs and two back legs, a large body and a smaller head, with an almost human-looking face.

Sam had never seen anything like them before.

ST. JUDE'S HOSPITAL, TENNESSEE

It was usual for the busy hospital where Alice was training to be a hive of activity, but for the last two days, due to spider bites, the emergency department staff had been run off their feet.

The spider bites were becoming more deadly, and some people were losing the use of their limbs after being bitten.

The public began to panic.

These spiders were making their mark everywhere.

People became paranoid, and even the minutest spiders were being sought out and killed.

CHAPTER 4

It was warm and cloudless in Kilkerry Park, and daylight was holding well into the evening.

Young Erica and her mother were playing catch ball when the ball suddenly flew past Erica and into the bushes behind her.

She turned and ran into the bushes to retrieve the ball.

After a few seconds, she came out screaming.

"Mummy, mummy, there's a monster in there."

The spider quickly scuttled away.

Erica was going through the monster stage, so the monster story was nothing new to her mother.

Mother felt exasperated but tried to be patient.

"Erica, I keep on telling you, there are no monsters," she said.

Erica would not be consoled, still insisting that she saw a monster.

That same evening, in Kilkerry Park, Harry Stacy, an old vagrant, bedded down for the night on the warm park bench.

No worries about feeling cold tonight.

He soon drifted into a deep sleep.

The next morning, a park maintenance worker found him dead.

How he died was a complete mystery until an autopsy revealed a large bite on his head.

The pathologist was baffled and amazed to find that the man's body had been completely drained of blood.

The findings leaked out, and the TV, newspapers, and radio proclaimed that the hunt was now on for killer spiders.

Of course, it was completely true and not just a far-fetched newspaper story.

The renegade spiders were now in epidemic form, and they were venting their spleen all over the country.

No area was immune from their deadly rampage.

At the airport, Captain Peter Wilson checked his bag before he took command of the jumbo jet bound for an international destination.

As he put his hand into the bag, the spider struck and rendered his arm completely useless.

While he was nursing his wound, not really realizing what had happened, the spider quickly exited the bag to carry on searching for more prey.

All kinds of transport began to be searched in fear, and to no avail.

Although the spiders were growing larger, they had the amazing ability to reduce their size and conceal themselves until they were ready to strike.

The attacks were being carried out in public places, and so far, there had been no reports of attacks in the home.

Ironically, babies, kindergarten, and Grade 1 children were not affected, and groups of kids at schools began going on spider hunts.

They were not afraid, and to them, it was fun and a great adventure.

Their parents were horrified to hear this and began keeping them home from school.

Working mothers took leave of absence from their jobs, and it became evident that the whole country was being brought to a standstill in more ways than one.

Ships carrying cargo for export were delayed for days while they were thoroughly searched.

CHAPTER 5

High-pitched, hysterical screams could be heard all over the

Manchester Hotel.

Nobody could pinpoint where they were coming from.

Suddenly, the screaming stopped.

Everyone listened intently.

"What the hell was that?" muttered one patron.

He received no reply only puzzled and inquiring stares.

The only sound to be heard was the sound of the elevator doors opening onto the ground floor after it had steadily made its way from the 10th floor.

The sight to be seen was gruesome and horrifying.

Four people lay dead on the floor, three men and one woman, arms and legs straddled in different directions.

Their grotesquely contorted faces looked like death masks, white and completely drained of blood.

The spiders had struck again, although the inhabitants of the hotel had no idea what had happened.

The spiders did their usual disappearing act, and the autopsy revealed spider bites on the victims' heads.

Since the smaller spiders were killed and taken to Sam Mason's lab, no other spiders had been caught.

A sensationalizing newspaper reporter got the idea that vampires really do exist and that was likely to be the explanation for the draining of blood, not spider bites.

The theory that a network of human vampires were the culprits soon hit the newspapers, which terrified the public even more.

Meanwhile, the spiders continued to strike.

Weird messages were being directed over the airways.

TV and radio programs were suddenly interrupted by a deep monotone voice saying, "we almost have complete control" and "keep to the plan; we are almost there."

But what did the messages mean? Everyone was puzzled.

TV and radio technicians had no explanation for the messages.

A few days later, another message was broadcast.

The voice said, "Now begin phase two."

This message was just as puzzling as the others had been.

After this message, attacks started to happen in homes and were just as deadly as all the others.

CHAPTER 6

One evening, Charlie felt unwell when he left for work, but hoped that the feeling would wear off as the night went on.

By 2:30 a.m., he felt worse and decided to go home.

The whole house was still and silent as Charlie quietly opened the back door, expecting to find ma sitting in the big armchair, reading.

His parents always slept with their bedroom door open, and for once, ma was sleeping like a baby.

John never had any problems sleeping.

Ma always said that he could sleep on a clothesline if he had to.

With hardly a sound, Charlie crept up the stairs, deliberately missing the creaky ones, with the delicacy of a Shaolin monk, making sure he did not disturb his mother.

The softly lit landing light was always left on, and as he approached the top of the stairs, he could see into his parents' bedroom.

He was startled to see an infrared beam suddenly shoot from the corner of the ceiling down toward his father's head.

It was being dispensed by the largest spider he had ever seen.

Luckily, John suddenly turned over, and the beam hit the pillow.

"Dad!" Charlie screamed as he rushed into the bedroom.

By the time his parents awoke, the spider had swiftly and deviously disappeared.

Clearly, Charlie had entered the house at just the right time.

But was it a spider? Charlie questioned.

It was interrupted while trying to complete its deadly act.

The infrared beam was the method the spiders sometimes used to stun their victims before they attacked.

Charlie caught a quick glimpse of its face, so human-looking, he could hardly believe what he saw.

John and Jean were stunned and appalled as Charlie related the event.

They felt sorry that he was sick, but at the same time glad, because otherwise, he wouldn't have been there to help them, and they could only guess what the consequences could have been.

Charlie and his father took their rifles out of the store and loaded them.

The three of them searched every nook and cranny in the house, but there was no sign of the spider.

Because it had been detected, it had exited the house, making its way to some other innocent victim.

For the next few nights, Jean and John took turns sleeping. The one not sleeping sat with a rifle across his or her lap, just in case the spider showed up again.

They finally figured that it wasn't coming back, so they went back to their normal sleeping routine.

CHAPTER 7

THE WHITE HOUSE

LATE AUGUST, 10 A.M. MONDAY

As the president sat at his desk, reviewing important matters,

he received a strange but explicit phone call.

The caller relayed a message.

"I am Tigon, leader of the spider nation.

"By now, it must be clear to you and everyone else what our

intentions are.

"We are going to rule your country and eventually the whole earth.

"By taking human blood, we have obtained your DNA structure and your intelligence and emotions, except the feelings of remorse and love.

"They have no place in our society.

"We are now almost ready to complete our transformation into human form.

"Your only chance to prevent more deaths is to give us complete control and inform your people of this decision.

"You may be wondering why this is happening.

"While your country has been nuclear testing, we have almost been annihilated.

"Almost, but not quite.

"You did not consider affairs of nature when you set out on your deadly course.

"Some of us survived, and now we intend to be the rulers and make sure that your madness never occurs again."

The president was almost speechless and astounded as he stuttered, "I-I can't make a decision just like that. I have to consult with my advisors first."

"You really don't have a lot of choice," said the voice. "I will give you two full days to make the inevitable decision. In the meantime, more people will die."

The president had to come up with a solution quickly, but what?

His thoughts were in turmoil as he called an emergency meeting.

CHAPTER 8

Ma was busy in the kitchen, making the family favorite, chocolate-chip cookies, which were always devoured in no time.

She never complained about that.

Baking and cooking for her family always made her feel needed and appreciated.

John sat drinking his coffee and reading the paper.

On the first ring of the telephone, he lifted the receiver.

Ma noted the startled expression on his face.

"It's Sheena. She's crying. I can hardly make out what she's saying. She wants to talk to you."

He anxiously looked at ma as she took the receiver.

"Calm down, Sheena, and try to speak slowly," she said.

"Oh, ma, Tom's in jail for murder," she sobbed.

Ma was flabbergasted.

"What?" She questioned. "What are you talking about? What's happened?"

"His secretary was found dead, and they're blaming him," she blurted out through her tears. "Oh, ma, what can I do? I know he didn't kill her."

Ma made a snap decision.

She and John would make the long drive to be with Sheena and the kids.

It was all they could do.

The boys would have to fend for themselves while they were away.

"Tom's finally done it," said ma as she related the story to John. "I knew women would be his downfall one day. I don't know why she's stayed with him so long."

"It's out of our hands, Jean. We can't make her do what we think she should do. She has to live her own life and take the consequences."

Ma knew, of course, that despite her reasoning, John was absolutely right.

The first heavy rainstorm of the summer decided to occur as they were heading to Sheena's place, causing their journey to be somewhat hazardous.

It took longer than it normally did, and they reached their destination in the late evening.

The kids were sleeping, and Sheena had just awakened from an emotionally exhaustive sleep.

She felt consoled and comforted as she greeted her parents.

Hugging them for a long time, she cried again.

Eventually, she was able to relate the whole story to them.

"Tom usually takes his secretary with him when he is negotiating a new job.

"This time, they had to go out of town, and they checked into a hotel as Mr. and Mrs. Bradford.

"The next morning Tom found her dead.

"I'm so confused," she said. "I thought he'd changed.

"Maybe it's the first time he's called another woman his wife. I don't know. But if he gets off the murder charge, I'm not sure what I'll do.

"I know I can't go on living like this, never being able to trust him."

John and Jean listened quietly, and Jean resisted the temptation to tell Sheena that she'd warned her about Tom before they were married.

John decided it was time for a course of action.

"Have you hired a lawyer yet?" He asked Sheena.

"No," she said. "I've been so upset, I haven't been able to think straight.

"Trying to explain to the kids hasn't been easy. Whatever he's done, he's still their dad, and they love him."

"Well, we'll find a lawyer first thing in the morning." said John. "We'll soon get this thing sorted out." He smiled and held his daughter's hand, trying to reassure her.

Sheena felt closer to her parents than she had ever felt before. It was a relief that she didn't have to deal with the situation all by herself.

CHAPTER 9

<u>THE WHITE HOUSE</u>

It was the first morning of the two days the president was given to make a decision.

He and his advisors agreed that they could not afford to play for time, but also that they couldn't possibly give in to these monsters.

So what was the solution?

Over the radio and TV during that morning came another puzzling message.

"Now begin phase three," said the voice.

What were they talking about?

Only the voice and his subjects understood.

At the airport, the huge jumbo was just about ready for take off.

The plane, destination UK, was full to capacity with excited and nervous people, some never having flown before.

Unknown to the crew and passengers, there were some uninvited, nonpaying passengers bedded down in the cargo hold.

They would not be welcome in the passenger seats.

Planes and ships scheduled for worldly destinations would be boarded by these unwanted creatures.

Nothing would be immune.

The president and his advisors were still in a quandary, trying to deal with the situation.

CHAPTER 10

Psychics and their abilities are not always considered to be dependable consultants, but as a last resort, the president decided to call on the services of one of the world's most renowned psychics.

The spiders had now taken on human characteristics, but they had overlooked the necessity to learn to swim, which made them very vulnerable.

The psychic told the president that he had to relay a message on TV and radio, because that was the way the creatures were communicating.

They would all hear this and do what was asked of them, because they were creatures of discipline.

Broadcasts would be made on every aircraft and ship, so they would all hear this message.

Numerous swimming pools would be emptied and dried out.

The unsuspecting spiders would be asked to congregate in the pools, which would be used as a forum.

A TV would be installed in each forum, and the creatures would officially see and hear the president hand over control of the country to them.

Hidden would be several large hoses, ready to be turned on them.

While that was happening, the pools would quickly start filling up, and they would be drowned.

The plot sounded cruel and sadistic.

The president was neither of those things, but if that was a sure way to defeat the spiders, then it had to be carried out.

After hearing this plan, the president and his advisors felt confident that they would soon eliminate the spiders.

At last, a solution had been presented to them.

Nothing could possibly go wrong. It would be completely straightforward.

Work was started on wording the message correctly.

The spiders must not suspect a thing. It must all sound very genuine.

Swimming pools all over the country were being drained and prepared for the most unusual ensemble that there had ever been.

The plan must not fail.

All of humanity depended on its success.

The submissive message was broadcast every hour to make sure that the entire spider nation received it.

Synchronization was the key.

The plan was finally carried out, and it worked like a charm.

At last, Tigon and his nation were destroyed, and the country was still under government control.

The triumph over the spider nation was then broadcast to the whole country.

Many bonfires were lit, celebrating the defeat.

But unknown to anyone, some of the spiders were trapped in the cargo hold of aircraft that were waiting for passengers and luggage to board.

The TV and receptors were still in place, and the spiders heard the triumphant message from the president.

They were devastated on hearing that their nation had been eradicated.

As the airport staff opened the luggage holds, thinking that everything was now safe, the spiders swiftly exited the planes undetected.

They were out for revenge.

They were going to get the president and make him pay for what he had done.

CHAPTER 11

It was late evening in the white house.

The president was at his desk, studying some notes.

After they had gained entry into the white house, completely unnoticed, the spiders moved cautiously and determinedly made their way to his study.

The door to the study was always left open, so they had no problem entering.

The president had relieved his secretary for the evening and was alone.

The spiders moved quickly.

Their leader sent out the infrared beam, completely stunning the president into silence.

They carefully and methodically started to engulf him in a shiny, fine silk thread.

This was the largest web they had ever spun.

The president sat there in his chair, still stunned and cocooned artistically in the spiders' masterpiece.

Their leader decided they would not kill him, not yet, anyway.

They could afford to play for time.

They had the upper hand.

Now the country would have to give in to them.

There was no other course they could take.

They made it perfectly clear that they would kill the president if they did not get what they wanted.

Once again, the country was in a dilemma and in the grip of

Unscrupulous, subhuman, unfeeling killers.

The president's advisors were at a loss what to do for the best.

The first instinct was to have soldiers break into the study and kill the spiders, but they knew that would not be as cut-and-dried as it sounded.

The spiders were very fast, and the president would be killed immediately.

If they were going to be destroyed, they would make sure they took him with them.

They would get revenge.

He was responsible for the murder of their nation.

CHAPTER 12

Just how patriotic is the president?

The question arose.

Would he choose to die rather than hand over the country to these monsters?

His advisors knew that this was the only acceptable solution, and it would surely work.

This situation was one that had reared its ugly head many times in war, when one person had to be sacrificed to save many.

Could the president's advisors be so callous?

That would be cold-blooded murder.

It might not have been such a difficult decision if the president had not been a family man.

He had a lovely young wife and three beautiful children.

How could they bring such grief to them?

The worst, but most acceptable solution would be to feign defeat, and allow the enemy to take control temporarily. Allow them to think that they were the victors until another plan could be assembled to destroy them.

Because most of their nation had been killed by a devious plan, the spiders would be very suspicious of anything and anyone who might contribute to their downfall.

The president's men and the FBI would have to make sure that no plans leaked out.

Two days after the president was taken captive, the spiders were informed by phone of the decision to hand over the country to them.

They were very wary and made it clear that they would have to keep the president captive until they were sure that everything was in place and completely under their control.

Now they were multiplying at an alarming rate and growing bigger.

Some of the females were already pregnant when they took over the white house.

Their first job was to form their own cabinet, and they realized the enormity of the job they had taken on.

There was so much to do, so much to consider.

Running a country successfully would not be an easy task.

The plan was to put their "people" in control in every state and municipality.

They were more human-looking now than ever, but their laws and general way of running things would not be the same as the humans.

They expected to receive much opposition and rebellion.

They would have to make people understand that they were in charge.

Everyone would realize what it was like to be at the mercy of a nation that did not consider other beings and lifestyles.

Humans had not learned to live and let live.

Now it was time for a taste of their own medicine.

CHAPTER 13

The .president would be held captive for quite some time.

The web around him had been removed, and food and drink were brought to him by request.

As long as the humans conformed to their wishes, the president was safe.

He knew this, but that did not stop him fearing that he might be killed at any time, at the spiders' whim.

As they gradually took over each state and municipality, they held one prominent person hostage to make sure they received no opposition.

Just as the humans had done, they had to set up their own defense mechanism.

Their greatest strength was in their webs, which, strand by strand of the fibrous protein-based silk, was stronger than steel.

All over the country, security personnel lost their jobs. There was no need for them.

Where security was needed, large webs were spun — across doorways, across windows and anywhere security was required, making even guard dogs unnecessary.

If anyone attempted to trespass, they would be caught up in the largest, strongest web they had ever seen.

When they were found, they would be consumed just like an insect.

Webs that were not interfered with would simply be unhooked and put aside until needed again.

Warnings about the web security were broadcast all over the country.

People foolhardy enough to ignore the warnings were playing into the hands of death.

There was no second chance.

A person caught stealing from stores or any establishment risked having one finger cut off one hand. If the offense was repeated, their hand would be cut off.

Car speedsters would not be tolerated. Their cars would be taken away for an indefinite period.

Fortunately, these harsh punishments did not have to be carried out. The warnings were enough to deter any wrongdoers.

The spider nation made it clear that they were going to rule with an iron rod of discipline.

This callous regime was not acceptable and would have to be brought to an end as soon as a plan could be asserted.

Ironically, for the first time in years, the crime rate decreased dramatically, as everyone realized that the authoritarians were not to be messed with.

The country functioned much the same as before, as long as people obeyed all the new rules.

The digestive system of spiders is adapted exclusively to taking up liquid food, because they generally digest their prey outside the body and then suck the fluid.

All through the campaign to be the dominant species, they have survived the same way and consumed various insects.

Because they were now almost human, Tamon, their new leader, decided that they should all start trying to eat human food and leave flies and insects for the smaller, unchanged members of their species.

But not for a while. That would come later.

CHAPTER 14

While the spider conflict was going on, Sheena and her parents were waiting for the pathologist's report on Tom's secretary.

John had hired a lawyer, and they were expecting a long, drawn-out murder trial.

When they finally got the report, they were very surprised and relieved.

It proved that the secretary had died from a large spider bite on her head, and her body had been completely drained of blood.

Tom was immediately released from custody.

Now Sheena had a heart-wrenching decision to make.

Could she still live with Tom after this final humiliation?

She had the children to consider, and it wouldn't be an easy decision.

She still loved Tom, and the thought of a future without him terrified her.

CHAPTER 15

The spider nation gradually increased their grip and control of the country.

Since they had become more human-looking, their babies were being born with human characteristics.

From the beginning of the campaign, their goal was to be more human-like in every possible way, because they believed that human beings were the rulers of destiny and everything else on the planet.

Tamon decided that their ultimate goal would be to mate with humans. That would be the final and horrifying climax.

Through the assimilation of human blood and human DNA, they had all reached average human height and had developed a certain repulsive attraction.

They grew hair on their bodies, much the same as humans, and they were of slim build, their limbs being vaguely muscular. By now, as well as being the rulers, they were attempting to integrate with humans, to try to understand their logic.

They wanted to understand why there was so much hate and aggression among them.

Just like many human beings who like to live in peace, they would never be able to come up with an answer.

CHAPTER 16

 With her head held high, Jessica strolled nonchalantly down the street.

She was beautiful and blue-eyed. Her long, golden, bushy mane tossed about in the gentle, warm wind.

Her skimpy dress clung to her small, shapely body.

Tamon couldn't take his eyes off her as he watched the slow rise and fall of her full breasts and the deep plunge of her cleavage.

He felt a pleasant sensation in his loins that he was not familiar with.

He knew that he had to have her.

Jessica was completely unaware of Tamon's feelings for her.

As she walked past him, she looked into his face and noted that he was fairly attractive.

Up to now, she'd had no contact with the spider men.

Tamon thought he would follow her and let her know that he was attracted to her.

He hoped the feeling would be mutual.

Whether it was or not, he had decided that she would belong to him.

He felt tenderness and a wish to protect her that was completely alien to him.

He thought that these must be the feelings of love, the same as humans feel, feelings that he had never felt before.

As he came close to Jessica, he put his hand on her arm.

She immediately pulled away in surprise and alarm.

Then he quietly told her not to be afraid, how much he admired her and would like her to live and mate with him.

Strangely enough, she found that she was not afraid of him at all.

She felt a compelling attraction to him, which seemed to be out of her control.

Although they had never met before, she felt that she wanted to be with him forever.

As she gazed into his deep, dark, penetrating eyes, she told him she loved him. Then she felt the warmth of his arms close around her as he pressed her to his tall, slender frame.

Jessica told Tamon that before she could conceive his child, he would have to marry her in the traditional human way.

Tamon agreed and told Jessica that he would love her forever.

And so, the strange, unheard-of union between the two began.

Gradually, more and more spider men entered into relationships with human women.

While the fascination with the attractive spider men existed in the minds of many human women, this state of affairs was not acceptable to most of the human population, particularly the men.

All over the country, people were demonstrating their displeasure.

The spider people had hoped that eventually, all the humans would begin to like and accept them.

It was obvious that was not going to be the case.

They had overrun and gained control of the country in a remarkably short time, and the government still had not come up with another solution to conquer them.

CHAPTER 17

The versatile spider people had adopted and developed many human talents.

Their most amazing achievement was their technological ability, particularly space exploration.

For some time, they had been researching various planets.

They organized a space program to explore a little-known planet called Spedron, which was nestled deep in the Milky Way.

But why Spedron?

Why not explore Mars, Jupiter, Saturn, or any of the other well-known planets?

Spedron is small and insignificant and had never caught the interest of NASA or anyone else involved in space exploration.

Tamon couldn't explain why, but for some reason, he felt compelled to visit the planet.

The day came to embark on the special journey to Spedron.

The weather conditions were perfect, the crew were fit and ready, all instruments checked out OK, and it was all systems go.

As Tamon and his crew soared through the universe, he thought of Jessica and mentally kissed and held her.

He pictured his blonde, blue -eyed daughter, Reya, and his dark-haired, brown-eyed son, Amon.

Would he ever see them again?

Meanwhile, back in Nevada, Tom sadly and hesitatingly entered his lovely home.

Sheena sat alone at the kitchen table, staring into space.

As Tom sat down opposite her, their eyes met, and he could see all the hurt and unhappiness she was feeling.

He hadn't meant to hurt her.

To him, it was just a harmless, simple fling.

To Sheena, it was devastating.

He knew he loved her and their children more than ever now.

Would she take him back and give him another chance?

He was in danger of losing everything he cherished because he'd taken it all for granted.

He'd been too sure of himself.

He vowed that he would never be unfaithful again.

Sheena could see the guilt and remorse on his handsome face.

She felt the love and commitment as he put his arms around her tightly — arms that would always be for her only.

They kissed, and the love they had felt when they first met

flooded back.

She knew she had to forgive him and start living again.

CHAPTER 18

The space shuttle gently, but firmly, touched down on Spedron.

One by one, Tamon and his crew descended the steps and carefully felt the ground beneath their feet.

They were amazed and bewildered at what awaited them.

Their feet sank into long, almost emerald-green grass.

They looked up at a light blue sky and scattered white clouds.

An orange, blazing sun directed heat down onto them.

For a few minutes, they were puzzled and began to think that their calculations had been wrong and they had somehow returned to Earth.

Hundreds of people started walking toward them.

Leading them was an elderly man dressed in ceremonial regalia.

He stepped away from the crowd and walked toward Tamon.

"Welcome to Spedron," he said. "I am Galon, the leader of our people.

"We have been waiting for you for several decades.

"We have watched closely as other planets have been explored, and I am well pleased that only you and your crew decided on this venture.

"We do not want the humans here, and I am glad that they do not find us interesting enough to explore.

"I am old and tired, and my work here is done. I am ready to go to my resting place.

"Tamon, I have waited for you for so long because you are the one named to be our next leader.

"It is the order of things, and nobody else can take your place."

"But I don't understand!" exclaimed Tamon. "I have never been on this planet before.

"I have come from the planet Earth, and I belong there.

"My wife and children are there, and I must go back to them."

"No," said Galon. "You must bring your family and all our people back here. This is where you all belong.

"Many years ago, our people became very rebellious. They began to have little respect for each other.

"They had even less respect for our beautiful green planet.

"They polluted it in many ways, and it gradually began to die.

"Disease and new viruses became rampant, and there seemed to be no defense against them.

"The only way out was to find a new planet to inhabit.

"Planet Earth seemed to be the most similar and likely planet to go to.

"Unfortunately, an unknown virus that attacked DNA structure was already on board the spaceship carrying the crew and several of the Spedron citizens.

"During the flight to Earth, their bodies were changed into large spider-type bodies, with two front legs and two back legs.

"Their brains still functioned the same as before the bodily change.

"These facts were related to us by the crew when they reached Earth, and it seems that only the Spedron people were affected.

"The virus obviously cannot survive on planet Earth.

"We have waited a long time for you to become a Spedronite again, and I'm overjoyed that it has finally happened."

"But Spedron doesn't look as though it's sick or dead," Tamon said. "It looks very healthy and bright."

"We don't really understand what happened," said Galon.

"Miraculously, after our people left for Earth, everything got better.

"Maybe it was the virus that was to blame for the upheaval. We'll never really know.

"But I do know that we have a beautiful, clean, green planet for you to bring our people back to.

"You are very courageous and disciplined, Tamon, and there is nobody better than you to lead our people and keep them on the straight and narrow path."

"I understand," Tamon nodded.

He went to prepare for the journey back to the planet Earth.

CHAPTER 19

Tamon worried as he hurried to tell the story to Jessica because she might say that she didn't want to leave planet Earth.

He couldn't live without her now. What would he do?

He had promised Galon he would be back to lead his people.

Jessica was not surprised when he related his story.

Perhaps her ancestors had once lived on Spedron.

In fact, she and the children were excited at the prospect of going to live on a new planet.

She loved flowers, and the only thing she would ask for when they arrived on Spedron, would be a beautiful large house with a garden.

As Tamon and his nation journeyed back to Spedron, he was glad to be leaving planet Earth.

Earth was a replica of Spedron, and many bad things were happening: unknown viruses suddenly appearing, environmental problems and too many greedy people only interested in making lots of money at the expense of those less fortunate than themselves.

Could it be a question of history repeating itself, he wondered?

About the Author

The author and her husband have just celebrated their Golden Wedding Anniversary. She is the mother of four daughters, who in total has provided her with fourteen grandchildren.

During her children upbringing years she has told many tales in relation to Childrens' fantasies both to her daughters and grandchildren.

She has a vivid imagination and will delight her readers in this sinister story.

CPSIA information can be obtained at www.ICGtesting.com
Printed in the USA
LVOW10s0747250315

431850LV00001B/2/P

9 781418 421625